SCHOLASTIC INC.

New York Toronto London Auckland Sydney

ISBN 0-590-96824-6

 Published by Scholastic Inc., 555 Broadway, New York, NY 10012, by arrangement with Random House, Inc.

12 11 10 9 8 7 6 5 4 8 9/9 0 1/0

Printed in the U.S.A. 24

First Scholastic printing, September 1996

Our friend the sun
is high and bright.
It's not yet time
to say good night.

It still is day,
it seems to say,
there still is time
for us to play.

But now the sun
is riding low.
Its light is now
a rosy glow.

Time for our bath.
We get undressed.
Ma helps us start.
We do the rest.

**We suds our fur
and rinse our heads.
We're still not ready
for our beds.**

Mama dries us.
Ouch! we shout
as Papa combs
our tangles out.

Now we have to
brush our teeth.
The ones on top,
the ones beneath.
We brush and brush
and brush our teeth.

The moon comes out.
We notice that
it's sometimes thin
and sometimes fat.

Is now the time
to say good night?
Our friend the moon
says no, not quite.
It's not yet time
to say good night.

We have to put
our nighties on.
We're getting sleepy.
We stretch. We yawn.

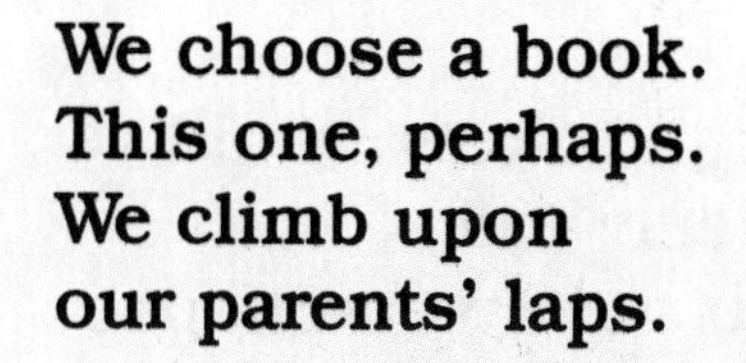
We choose a book.
This one, perhaps.
We climb upon
our parents' laps.

**Though others would
do nicely too--
which book you choose
is absolutely
up to you.**

Now the time
has come for dozing.
Even Papa's eyes
are closing.

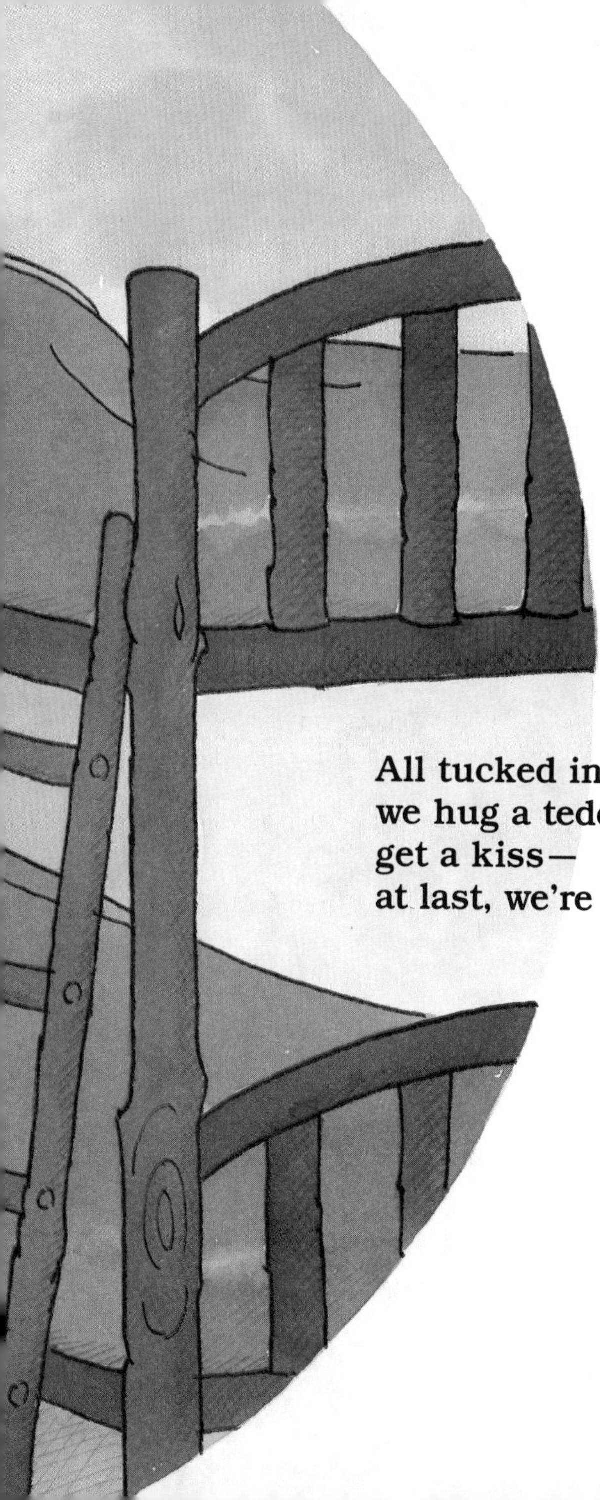

All tucked in,
we hug a teddy,
get a kiss—
at last, we're ready.

With the moon aglow,
the stars so bright,
it's time at last
to say good night.

Good night.
Good night.
Good night.
Good night.